Queen
and
King
Penguin

Smile

Fellow Armadillos

Thom Fox

Los Dos Flamingos

Alice,
the
Grey
Roo

Mr.
Wild
Boar

Betty,
the
Beluga
Whale

Edgar,
the
Blue-Toed
Tiger

© 1999, DOODLEZOO, LLC.
Written by Keith R. Potter
Color illustrations and computer artwork
by Keith R. Potter based on original line drawings by Jana Leo.
Research assistance provided by Ken Fulk.

Photographs (in order of appearance):
African grasslands, Digital Vision
Cheetah running at full speed, Karl Ammann/Corbis
Cheetah, Digital Stock
Cheetah, Digital Stock
Mother cheetah with cubs, Karl Ammann/Corbis
Adult cheetah with six month old cubs, Tom Brakefield/Corbis
Adult cheetah with six month old cubs, Tom Brakefield/Corbis
Lion in East Africa, The Purcell Team/Corbis
Pride of older lion cubs, Galen Rowell/Corbis
Lion and lioness, Joe McDonald/Corbis
Lioness and springbok, Digital Stock
Lionesses sleeping on each other, The Purcell Team/Corbis
Lioness leading her cubs, Peter Johnson/Corbis
Lionessess resting in a tree, Alissa Crandall/Corbis
Bengal tiger, PhotoDisc
Bengal tiger, National Geographic
Tiger resting in sun, Lynda Richardson/Corbis
A swimming tiger, Philip Marazzi; Papilio/Corbis
Bengal tigress with cubs, National Geographic
Bengal tiger walking on road, Mary Ann McDonald/Corbis

Book design by Keith R. Potter.
Typeset in Glypha and Crud font.
Printed in Singapore.

Library of Congress Cataloging-in-Publication Data available.

Distributed in Canada by Raincoast Books
8680 Cambie Street, Vancouver, British Columbia V6P 6M9

10 9 8 7 6 5 4 3 2 1

Chronicle Books
85 Second Street, San Francisco, California 94105

www.chroniclebooks.com/Kids

Cat nap

doodlezoo®

Written by
Keith R Potter

Illustrated by
Keith R Potter
and **Jana Leo**

chronicle books · san francisco

We are **Edgar, the Blue-Toed Tiger**, Ryan Lion and **Miss Cheetah**. Join us as we leave camp and set off to meet three of the world's most ferocious felines.

We are here to encounter cheetahs, lions, and tigers in their natural domain. Being curious little beasts ourselves, we simply must find out if these graceful, majestic, wild cats act anything like the little fluffy ones humans have at home.

For instance, do speedy **cheetahs** chase mice?

...Do mighty African **lions** purr?

...Do furry Bengal **tigers** cough-up gigantic hairballs?

...And, most importantly, do these big powerful pussy cats take nice, long, lazy, luxurious cat naps?

Lions! tigers! ...and cheetahs!

Oh my!

Quiet down! I think I see something racing toward us...

Cheetahs

Our adventure begins in **East Africa** on the wide open plains of the **Serengeti**. This is a protected area of dry grassland that is home to a large variety of wildlife...including the racy cheetah.

Cheetahs are **carnivores,** which means that like all cats they eat meat. (Freshly killed, still-on-the-bone, red, raw meat!)

To chase down a meaty meal, cheetahs rely on being quick. A hungry cheetah can reach speeds of up to 75 miles (112 kilometers) per hour. No other cat can outrun a cheetah. In fact, **cheetahs are the fastest land animals on the planet.**

Cheetah is a Hindi word meaning "spotted one."

Cheetahs used to live in India and across other parts of Asia. But because of hunting, and competition with humans for space, the number of cheetahs has greatly declined. Today, these rare beasts can only be found in a few spots in the Middle East and Africa.

We quickly discovered that cheetahs are sprinters, not long-distance runners. A cheetah can go from 0 to 45 miles (72 kilometers) per hour in two seconds flat. Most cheetahs can only keep up this kind of speed for about 500 yards (457 meters). They then must stop to catch their breath and cool down!

When he is moving fast those spots are a blur!

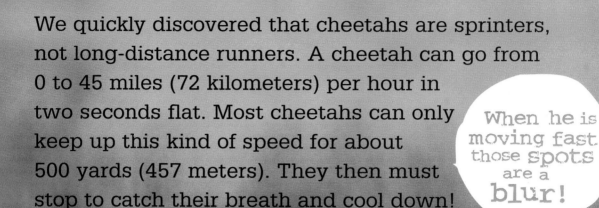

The black streaks on a cheetah's face are believed to help it see better.

They work like sunglasses, absorbing glare from the sun so a cheetah can see better while running fast.

Because **cheetahs are built for speed**, they look much different than other cats. They have lean bodies and long legs to help them move very fast.

They have very long tails which they use to help them steer and change direction. Cheetahs even have very flexible spines which bend and stretch as they run.

Cheetahs work hard to find and catch their food. Usually only one in ten chases is successful. They do most of their hunting during the day.

If the weather is hot, cheetahs will hunt in the early morning or early evening when it is cooler.

Most adult cheetahs **live and hunt alone**. They rely on keen eyesight to locate their food, usually **gazelles**, **antelopes**, and **wild boar**. If the pickings are slim, cheetahs will also eat smaller prey like birds and rabbits. A cheetah may even chase after a mouse. (But to a hungry cheetah a mouse is not a meal!)

Shhhh... Be very, very quiet ...we are on the prowl!

Purrfect sunset ...don't you think?

Adult cheetahs usually only come in contact with one another when it is time to mate. After courtship and mating, a **male cheetah** does not participate in raising the cubs. A **female cheetah** does all this work herself. Sometimes there are as many as seven hungry mouths to feed.

Young cheetah cubs are in constant danger. They must remain hidden and try to stay quiet when their mother is away hunting. Hyenas and lions will eat cheetah cubs. This mother cheetah hides her cubs by moving them to a new den every few days.

Cheetahs cannot roar like other big cats, instead cheetahs make chirping noises.

A mother cheetah will use a shrill chirp to call to her cubs.

Her cubs will chirp back when they are hungry or frightened.

By the time cheetahs are seven months old, they begin to hunt with their mother. At first, they watch from a safe distance. Later they make clumsy attempts to hunt by themselves.

Practice makes perfect. It will take many, many months of practice before these juvenile cubs will become **expert hunters**.

After a cheetah kills its prey, it must eat it quickly.

Nearby, lions and hyenas will attack a cheetah and steal its meal. A cheetah is no match for a hungry lion or a pack of hyenas.

This cheetah family won't be taking too many more long, lazy cat naps together.

By the time cheetahs cubs are eighteen months old, they are ready to take on the big bad world all by

themselves. And after a year and half, this mother will soon be ready to raise another litter.

A cheetah is often three years old before it has refined its hunting skills and claimed its own territory. During that time, which is called the dispersal stage, life can be very difficult.

Juvenile cheetahs risk starvation and serious injury because some never learn to hunt successfully.

Get up! Quickly! I just heard a lion roar ...and it was mighty loud.

ZzzZzz, ZZZ, ZzzZZzzZ (a lion, where?) zZzZz...

17

Lions

The African lion often lives alongside the cheetah on Africa's protected grasslands. These cats may share the same territory, but there are big

differences between lions and cheetahs. For example, unlike cheetahs, lions can let out a loud ear-splitting **roar**.

Lions greet one another with a purr like all cats do. But unlike smaller cats, lions, tigers, and leopards also roar.

A male lion will give a ferocious roar to keep away other male lions and to stop other animals from trespassing on his territory.

This low, rumbling, bone-shaking roar can be heard for many miles.

Most cats are solitary animals. Lions are the BIG exception. They are the only big cats that live together in large social groups. These groups are called **prides**. A pride includes many **lionesses** (females), their cubs, and one or more adult males.

Lions do most of their hunting at night. They must be able to see well in the dark to spot moving objects from far away. To do this, lions have very large eyes. Their eyes are larger than any other meat-eating animal.

The strongest, oldest adult male lion protects the pride. He roars a lot and chases off other male lions and bothersome scavengers like hyenas and wild dogs. Occasionally, two or more males will share the duties of ruling a pride.

An adult male lion spends most of his time trying to take over a pride of lions or defending his own pride from being taken over.

A lion may rule over a pride for just a few months or for several years, depending on how big and strong he is, and how good he is at defending his turf.

While he is **king of the beasts** (or at least, ruler of his own pride), a male lion mates with any female lion ready to have cubs. But if a male approaches a lioness who is not quite ready, he will get a nasty swat across the face.

Has he no **pride?**

Sometimes a roar is not enough to scare off another male lion, and the pride leader will have to fight it out. A male lion's big, bushy mane offers some protection from bites and nasty claw swipes..

A mane also makes the adult male look larger than he actually is. Big hair all by itself may be enough to scare off younger male rivals.

Lionesses do most of the hunting. They are lighter and swifter than male lions. They don't have those big furry manes to get in the way, either.

Lionesses **work as a team** when they hunt. A group will **stalk** together through the tall grass. Once they select their target they fan out and surround their prey. At this point, one lioness begins the chase. She forces the startled animal to run toward another member of the pride, who is ready **pounce**.

Looks like it's **supper time!**

Time for a little frisky buffet.

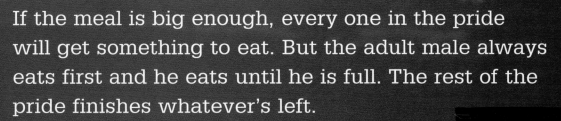

If the meal is big enough, every one in the pride will get something to eat. But the adult male always eats first and he eats until he is full. The rest of the pride finishes whatever's left.

Because they hunt in groups, lions are the only cats that often kill animals bigger than themselves. Only rhinoceroses, hippos, and elephants are large enough to relax comfortably around a pride of lions.

Made with 100% antelope and antelope by-products!

All cats have rough tongues.

The rough bumps on a cat's tongue are called papillae. Cats use their tongues to groom themselves. They also use their tongues like sharp steak knives to rip and scrape meat off of bones. Cats do not have the teeth necessary to chew food. They swallow chunks of raw meat whole.

Lions do not hunt every day. Especially if they have eaten a huge meal. Lions have been known to eat as much as 60 pounds (27 kilograms) of meat in one feeding. After a meal like that, lions are stuffed full.

At this point, they often do nothing more than take a big, long, lazy cat nap. **Lions are very fierce nappers.** These big cats sleep about 20 hours a day!

ZzzZzz, ZZZ, ZzzZzz, zZzZz...

From birth until lion cubs are six to eight weeks old, they have dark spots on their fur. The spots help the cubs hide in the underbrush, keeping them safe from predators like leopards and hyenas, while the lionesses in the pride are out hunting.

The spots gradually disappear. By the time a lion cub is four or five months old it will have its sleek, virtually spotless, adult coat.

When it is time for a lioness to give birth, she leaves her pride. She finds a hidden **den** where she gives birth to usually two to three cubs. Lion cubs, just like domesticated kittens, are **born blind** and helpless. They spend the first few weeks in the den sleeping and feeding on their mothers's milk.

Until the cubs are old enough to get about on their own, the mother will carry them around by the scruff of the neck. By the time cubs are six weeks old they can walk and follow behind their mother. At this point the family rejoins their pride.

Young male lions leave the pride when they are between three and four years old. Until they can find their own pride, they will wander alone or with other young single males.

Lionesses usually remain with the same pride all their lives. Most females in a pride are closely

related. A pride is made up of mothers, daughters, sisters, aunts, grandmothers, and nieces....

A cat's claws are an important tool and weapon. Just like little house cats, big wild cats, like lions, must keep their claws sharp and clean.

A lion will scratch on a nearby tree with its claws to sharpen and clean them. A little house cat may scratch on a nearby sofa.

ZzzZzZ (nice slumber party!), ZzzZzz, zZzZz...

Wake up!... Nap time is over. It's tiger tracking time!

Tigers

On our final stop, we journey deep into India's jungles in search of the secretive and rare **Bengal tiger**.

Tigers are the **biggest** of all big cats. A male Bengal tiger grows to about 9 1/2 feet (2.9 meters) long and

There were once eight
known types (species)
of tigers living in
the wild.

The Caspian, Bali, and
Javan tigers have
become extinct. The
Bengal, South China,
Indochinese, Sumatran,
and Siberian tigers,
still exist in the wild.

All five species are
very rare and each is
in grave danger of
becoming extinct.

Today, more tigers live
in cages and perform
in circus acts than live
free in the wild.

weighs about 450 pounds (204 kilograms). A female, called a **tigress**, can grow up to 8 1/2 feet (2.6 meters) and weigh about 300 pounds (136 kilograms).

In a dense forest or a thick jungle a tiger can be very hard to see. A **tiger's stripes** help to hide it from its prey. Tiger stripes are **disruptive camouflage**, which means that the stripes make it difficult to see the entire tiger.

Tigers very carefully and silently stalk their prey. Once they are close enough they will wait in ambush, hiding low in the tall grass. When a meal, usually deer or gaur (wild cattle), gets within striking distance, a tiger will charge and pounce on it.

Just as no two humans have the same fingerprints, no two tigers have the same stripes.

Scientists, trying to count how many tigers are alive in the wild, are able to tell one tiger from another by their unique stripes.

Each tiger has its own **territory** where it lives and hunts. Tigers need a large space filled with lots of animals to hunt. The average tiger eats 7000 pounds (3175 kilograms) of meat a year.

Adult tigers avoid contact with each other. They use their roars and scent markings (picture a dog and a fire hydrant!) to stay in touch. In order to survive in the wild it is important that tigers minimize conflict with one another.

An adult male tiger's territory is usually about 11 square miles (30 square kilometers). This area encompasses the smaller ranges of several females with whom a male will breed.

Males are usually only strong enough to defend their home range for about two to four years. Older tigers who lack their own territory are the ones that usually resort to eating domestic cattle or even humans.

ZzzZzZ (finally I get a nap), ZzzZzz, zZzZz...

Unlike cheetahs and lions, tigers, like to swim, soak, and bathe in the water.

Tigers are great swimmers, but they almost never get their heads wet. It is important that tigers can always see, smell, and hear what is going on around them. Tigers even enter the water tail first to make sure they keep their heads dry.

It is important that a tiger have a nice cool stream, river, or lake in his territory. At the height of the dry season it is very hot (115°F/47°C) and Bengal tigers need to swim and soak to cool off.

Tigers know that other animals need water, too. Tigers hide themselves in the nearby tall grass

and wait quietly for dinner to come down to the watering hole for a drink.

If a tiger pounces on a deer or some other prey while it's in the water, it must be careful. Crocodiles are just below the surface. Crocodiles will grab the tiger's meal and maybe even the tiger itself!

A tigress will usually have a **litter** of three to four cubs. At three to four months tiger cubs are ready to eat meat. Not until they are twelve to sixteen months will tiger cubs learn to hunt.

In their natural environment, wild cats, like tigers, get plenty of dietary fiber from plants, feathers, hair, and beaks. Raw meat provides essential fatty acids.

Both fiber and fatty acids help tigers maintain very strong digestive systems. As a result, big cats in the wild have little problem with digesting bones and cartilage. And, unlike domestic cats, tigers rarely cough-up hairballs.

yeah... My stomach is a bit queasy.

Like all kittens, tiger cubs spend most of their waking hours playing games. Cat play helps cubs grow strong and lets them practice skills that they will soon need to survive as adults in the wild.

Our bungle in the jungle had come to an end. It's a good thing because we were completely exhausted. Bushed. Dog tired.

We three kitties were ready for a cat nap.

As we headed out of the steamy jungle, we reflected on everything we had seen and learned about the BIG cats. Somehow though, the three of us understood we had only scratched the surface.